GW00499323

Frank Muir
Illustrated by Joseph Wright

First published 1986 by A & C Black (Publishers) Ltd
35 Bedford Row, London WC1R 4JH

Photoset in Garamond by Tunbridge Wells Typesetting Services
Printed in Portugal by Resopal

British Library Cataloguing in Publication Data
Muir, Frank
What-a-Mess has breakfast.
I. Title II. Wright, Joseph, 1947-
823'.914 [J] PZ7
ISBN 0-7136-2858-8

A & C BLACK · LONDON

It is a well-known fact that the tummy of a young puppy is one of the nicest things in nature.

When a puppy rolls on its back, pale pink skin shines through its silky baby-fur and when you touch the tummy it is like stroking warm velvet.

This is true of all puppies—except for one; the noble Afghan hound puppy whose real name was Prince Amir of Kinjan but who was known to everybody, for very good reasons, as What-a-Mess.

What-a-Mess's tummy was certainly not for tickling that Saturday morning. The wet cement he had rolled in had dried but the hair on his tummy had stiffened into hard spikes, like a downward-pointing punk hair-cut.

And What-a-Mess was hungry. So his tummy, far from being pink and peaceful, was making little squeaking noises. As though a tiny, fairy motor-cyclist was roaring round the puppy's insides on a miniature Honda. "Wheeeeoooo" went the tummy. And then, as the tiny motor-cyclist revved round another bend, "Woooooaaaaaa!"

What-a-Mess searched the drawing-room for scraps. He attacked the big sofa, hurling the cushions on the floor and rummaging with his long nose into the corners. He found a rather hairy half-chewed toffee and ate it but, as his tummy reminded him, that could hardly be called a meal.

Alas, there was nothing for What-a-Mess to eat. The family had gone away for the whole day, taking his mother with them. What-a-Mess had to stay behind. "Good things," his mother explained to him, "happen to *good* dogs, and you have been a very naughty dog indeed."

Not only had he spoilt the new cement path which the man had spent all day laying but he had also eaten his own dog-basket, a nibble a night, until none of it was left. And he had gone to sleep in the middle of the pavement outside the gate and the nice old lady next door had trodden on him and dropped the new-laid eggs she was taking to a friend.

The family had left the puppy plenty of food, of course. Puppies have four meals a day so they had put four bowls of food on the floor for him. One bowl with his breakfast in it, one with his lunch, one with his tea, and a little one with his supper.

But when the family had departed, very early, What-a-Mess had felt so sad at being locked up in the house all alone that he had enjoyed a little mournful bark and then eaten up the whole four bowls of food.

That was hours ago and now he was hungry again. And there was no food left. Not a fragment of biscuit in any of the bowls. Not a smear of nourishing marrowbone jelly.

"Beeeeeeuuuuup!" gurgled his tummy, which the puppy knew from experience meant "Where's breakfast?"

He decided to try upstairs.

In the bathroom he found a cupboard full of bottles. He climbed up and stood on the basin to find whether they were full of food but he slipped and the bottles cascaded into the basin and broke.

The smell reminded him of visits to the vet so he quickly jumped down.

One of his paws landed on a tube of toothpaste and a long, pink ribbon of stuff smelling of peppermint shot out across the floor and up the wall. What-a-Mess tried a lick. It tasted quite nice so he licked up a length of it.

His mouth began to foam. The puppy caught sight of himself in the mirror and he seemed to have a pink moustache and beard like a tinted Father Christmas.

He decided that the best way to get rid of the foam was to run fast and let the wind blow it away. He raced off down the corridor at tremendous speed.

Flecks of pink froth flew off his face and stuck to the walls. Down the stairs he shot, five at a time, and sped into the drawing-room, leaping high over the back of the sofa like a champion steeplechaser.

Several things then happened quickly.

The fat puppy thudded down onto the sofa springs. They acted like a trampoline and bounced him up again. He flew through the air, hit the French windows and they burst open.

He landed with a dull thud on a bag of cement lying on the grass. The bag burst. A dense cloud of fine powder rose into the air and then gently settled, covering What-a-Mess.

Slowly and painfully the now chalk-white puppy dragged himself down the gravel path and lay down by the gate. "That does it!" he said to himself. "Nothing but nasty things have happened this morning so from now on I am going to be really *good.* Then nice things will happen. Mummy promised. I shall be the well-behaved, Devoted Family Pet, weak from lack of breakfast but loyally waiting at the gate all day for his beloved family to return . . ." He sighed and closed his eyes.

At that moment the nice old lady from next door was making her way along the pavement, trying for the second time to deliver food to her friend. She loved animals and was worried about having accidentally trodden on What-a-Mess. "Such a young puppy," she muttered. "I could have hurt him. Perhaps badly . . ."

At that point she passed the gate and glanced in. There, lying on the gravel, was a strangely white dog.

"THE GHOST OF WHAT-A-MESS!!!" she cried, flinging up her hands—and the goodies in them—and running as fast as she could back to her house.

The puppy opened his eyes at the noise. There was nobody there. But suddenly a number of objects began to drop from the sky and fall to the ground near his nose: a large packet of bacon, a chunk of mellow cheese, a bar of chocolate . . .

"My mother was right," thought What-a-Mess, carefully wrapping half a bar of chocolate in four slices of bacon and balancing on top a piece of cheese, a blob of strawberry jam and a broken egg. "Good things *do* happen to you when you're good. Even, it seems, when you're good for only about a minute!"

He took a trial lick. His tummy purred.

What-a-Mess had breakfast.